The Case of the Missing Movie

Look for these Clue™ Jr. books!

The Case of the Missing Movie

Book created by Parker C. Hinter

Written by Della Rowland

Illustrated by Sam Viviano

Based on characters from the Parker Brothers game

A Creative Media Applications Production

SCHOLASTIC INC.
New York Toronto London Auckland Sydney

No part of this publication may be reproduced in whole or in part, or stored in a retrieval system, or transmitted in any form or by any means, electronic, mechanical, photocopying, recording, or otherwise, without written permission of the publisher. For information regarding permission, write to Scholastic Inc., 555 Broadway, New York, NY 10012.

ISBN 0-590-26218-3

Copyright © 1995 by Waddingtons Games Ltd.
All rights reserved. Published by Scholastic Inc. by arrangement with Parker Brothers, a division of Tonka Corporation. CLUE® is a registered trademark of Waddingtons Games Ltd. for its detective game equipment.

12 11 10 9 8 7 6 5 4 3   5 6 7 8 9/9 0/0

Printed in the U.S.A.   40

First Scholastic printing, August 1995

Contents

Introduction

Meet the members of the Clue Club.

Samantha Scarlet, Peter Plum, Georgie Green, Wendy White, Mortimer Mustard, and Polly Peacock.

These young detectives are all in the same fourth-grade class. The thing they have most in common, though, is their love of mysteries. They formed the Clue Club to talk about mystery books they have read, mystery TV shows and movies they like to watch, and also, to play their favorite game, Clue Jr.

These mystery fans are pretty sharp when it comes to solving real-life mysteries, too. They all use their wit and deductive skills to crack the cases in this book.

1

You can match *your* wits with this gang of junior detectives to solve the eight mysteries. Can you guess who did it? Check the solution that appears upside down after the story to see if you were right!

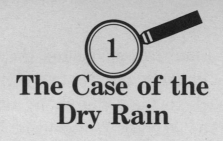

The Case of the Dry Rain

"**O**h, no! Not today!" Polly Peacock moaned as she looked outside her bedroom window. It was raining.

Polly picked up her pet turtle and carried him to the window. "This is your kind of weather, Speedo," she said to the turtle. "Wet!"

Today was definitely a bad day for rain. It was the Fourth of July. And tonight, everyone in town was going to Flannel's Field to watch the fireworks display. "I wonder if the fireworks will be canceled because of the rain," Polly said to Speedo.

The Clue Club had planned to watch the show together. Mortimer Mustard had complained that his neck always hurt when he watched fireworks. He hated looking up at the sky for so long.

Peter Plum had suggested they spread a blanket on the grass. That way they could all lie back to view the show. Samantha Scarlet and Wendy White were bringing blankets, and Georgie Green had said he had a sleeping bag.

Now what would they do? Polly picked up the phone and called Peter.

"Can you believe this weather?" Polly complained.

"I know," sighed Peter. "It's been beautiful all week. Blue skies. No clouds. And today it rains!"

"Have they ever called off the Fourth of July fireworks?" asked Polly. "I mean, can they? Can you give the Fourth of July a rain date?"

"I don't know," said Peter. "Other national holidays aren't celebrated on the actual dates. They're celebrated on the closest Monday."

"That's right," agreed Polly. "I have a hard time remembering when Washington's and Lincoln's birthdays really are.

4

But at least we always get a long week-end."

"Well, I've celebrated my birthday on other days," Peter said. "I guess I'd tell George and Abe that it's not so bad."

"But what about the country's birth-day?" repeated Polly. "I never heard of fireworks on the fifth of July."

"Maybe the rain will stop and we won't have to worry," sighed Peter. "Listen, I just talked to Mortimer. The rest of the club is at his house playing Clue Jr. Why don't we go over there, too?"

"Okay," said Polly. "See you soon."

Mortimer's house was the perfect place to be on a rainy day. He had a large base-ment with cable TV, a Ping-Pong table, and other games. He even had a small re-frigerator full of soft drinks. When Peter and Polly arrived, the rest of the kids were in the middle of a game of Clue Jr.

"Come on in, guys," said Mortimer. "We're almost through with this game. You can get in on the next one."

"Mrs. Mustard said we could have a picnic down here," Wendy said. "She told us a little rain won't stop us from having a Fourth of July picnic."

"She said since we couldn't have one outside, we'd just have one inside!" said Samantha.

"She's bringing the food down in a picnic basket," exclaimed Georgie. "We're having sandwiches and potato chips. She even made us brownies for dessert."

Georgie stopped talking and looked around. Mortimer looked mad. "Hey, what's wrong?" Georgie asked.

"You shouldn't talk about food when everyone's so hungry," Mortimer complained.

"Georgie always gets so excited when he's hungry," said Wendy.

"Not Mortimer," said Polly. "He gets grumpy." Everyone burst out laughing — everyone but Mortimer.

Just then, Mrs. Mustard called out, "Here's your picnic." Georgie and Mortimer raced up the stairs to carry down the basket.

Mortimer took a handful of chips and flipped on the cable weather channel. "Let's check the forecast while we eat," he said.

The forecaster on TV was pointing to a weather map. "Our weather satellite shows that the rain should end by early afternoon," she said. "That means the skies will clear up in time for this evening's fireworks display."

The kids sighed with relief. Sure enough, by the time they finished their picnic, the rain had stopped.

"Let's bike over to Flannel's Field to see if the fireworks show is still on," Peter said. Everyone nodded.

Georgie grabbed the picnic basket to carry upstairs. As everyone ran out the door, he called out, "Thanks for the picnic, Mrs. Mustard."

When the kids reached the field, they noticed a couple of boys in a tent. "Look," said Wendy, pointing to the boys. "There's Sid Rose and Johnny Brickman."

Sid and Johnny waved at the Clue Club kids, who raced over on their bikes.

Samantha rode around the tent, checking it out. "What a swell tent!" she exclaimed.

"Can we come in?" asked Mortimer.

"Sure," said Sid, pulling the front flap back. Everyone crowded into the tent. The tent had a canvas floor so everyone could sit down. It felt cozy inside.

"We're going to camp out tonight," Johnny told them. "We'll watch the fireworks, then sleep out under the stars. Cool, huh?"

"Great!" said Mortimer. "I love to camp out."

"Me too," said Peter. "Sometimes I stretch out in my backyard at night and try to find the constellations. Once I saw a shooting star. It was so neat, I did a science report on shooting stars. Did you know that a shooting star is actually a — "

Samantha interrupted. "Hopefully we'll be seeing shooting fireworks tonight," she said. Everyone knew if someone didn't say something quick, Peter would tell them everything he'd ever read about shooting stars. And Peter had read a lot about shooting stars.

"This is a nice tent," Polly told Sid and Johnny. "You even have a floor in it."

"Yeah, we put a tarp down so our sleeping bags wouldn't get wet," said Sid.

"That's right," said Wendy. "The grass is still wet. I guess we can't lie out on our blankets tonight."

"Why don't I bring the shower curtain Dad puts down on the floor when he paints?" suggested Peter. "It would keep the blankets from getting wet."

"Good idea," said Samantha. "We're all set."

"Let's go home and get our stuff," said Georgie. "We want to make sure we get a good spot for tonight."

10

"Right," said Mortimer. "And we need to pack some food, too."

Everyone ducked their heads as they came out of the tent.

"See you tonight," Sid said, as the kids got on their bikes.

Just then, a van pulled up. BLUEVILLE'S SPORTING GOODS was painted on the side. Mr. Blueville and a young woman got out.

"That's the kid," she said, pointing at Sid. "He's the one I saw this morning at your store. He stole the tent."

Mr. Blueville walked around Sid's tent, looking it over.

"Hi, Mr. Blueville," said Sid. "What are you doing here?"

"I hate to say this, son," said Mr. Blueville. "But this woman says she saw you running out of my store this morning. And you were carrying a tent."

"No way," said Sid to Mr. Blueville. "It couldn't have been me. I've been camping out in this tent since yesterday."

11

Johnny vouched for him. "We wanted to get a good view of the fireworks," he explained, "so we put the tent up early."

Mr. Blueville turned to the woman. "If these boys have been here since yesterday, this can't be my stolen tent," he said.

"I guess you must have seen someone who looks like me," Sid told the woman.

Just then Mortimer piped up. "Sid, your story is all wet and I can prove it."

How does Mortimer know that Sid isn't telling the truth?

Solution
The Case of the Dry Rain

"Whaaat?" cried Sid. "What are you talking about!"

"Your story is as wet as the ground underneath your tent," said Mortimer. "You and Johnny told us you put a tarp down on the ground so your sleeping bags wouldn't get wet."

"So?" said Johnny.

"I see," said Peter. "If they had put up their tent two days ago, then the ground underneath it would be dry."

Mr. Blueville pulled up the tarp. Sure enough, the ground underneath it was wet. When they saw they were caught, the boys confessed.

"They might have gotten away with this if it weren't for you," Mr. Blueville told the Clue Club.

"Looks like the rain this morning left Sid and Johnny high and dry," said Georgie.

2
The Case of the Winning Combination

BRRRRIIING!! The last morning school bell rang. Ms. Redding began taking attendance for her fourth-grade class.

"Does anyone know if Polly Peacock is sick?" she asked the class.

Peter Plum raised his hand. "She's here, Ms. Redding. I think she can't get her locker open."

"Again?" asked Ms. Redding. She turned to Georgie Green. "Georgie, could you see if Polly is in the hall for me?"

Georgie hurried to the hall where the fourth-grade lockers were. Sure enough, there was Polly fumbling at her locker. And she was mad.

"Ms. Redding sent me to look for you," said Georgie.

"This old lock is driving me crazy, Georgie," Polly muttered, gritting her teeth. "I can't get into my locker."

"Let me try to open it," Georgie told her. He spun the dial to the left, then right, then left again. Nothing happened. He tried again. No luck.

Georgie grabbed the lock and put one foot against the locker. Then he pulled hard on the lock a couple of times, making a banging noise.

Polly's eyes got big. "Georgie!" she whispered. "What are you doing?"

"Sometimes this works on mine," Georgie told her.

"Well, stop!" said Polly. "You'll break it! Plus, you're making all this noise."

He bent over and tried the combination again, but the lock still wouldn't open. "Well, so much for a physical solution," he said. "Why don't you ask Ms. Redding to have Mr. Gleamington change your lock?"

"Okay," Polly said. "I've been late to class twice this week because of it."

When Georgie and Polly returned to

class, Polly explained her problem to her teacher. Ms. Redding called Mr. Gleamington, the school janitor, over the intercom.

By the time Mr. Gleamington opened the locker and Polly got her books, half of first period was over. "Mr. Gleamington is going to fix your lock after school," Ms. Redding said to Polly. "Maybe if we get your locker fixed, we can get more math done."

At eleven-thirty, the lunch bell rang. The fourth grade hurried to their lockers to put away their books before going to the school cafeteria.

"This is the best period of the day," said Mortimer Mustard happily. "Not only do we have lunch, we play Clue Jr. while we eat."

One by one, the Clue Club gathered at Polly's locker while she tried to get her lock open again.

"The fourth-grade lockers must be the

oldest ones in the school," said Wendy White.

"They are the hardest to open," Samantha Scarlet said.

"Nobody can crack them," said Georgie, laughing at his joke.

Mortimer closed his locker and joined the others. He had an enormous lunch bag in one hand and his Clue Jr. game in the other.

"Hurry, Polly," said Mortimer. "I'm starving."

"Want me to try, Polly?" asked Peter.

"Be my guest," fumed Polly. At first Peter couldn't budge the old lock either, but after two more tries, he popped it open. Polly sighed with relief and threw her books up on the shelf inside.

"Okay, I'm ready," she said. She started to close the locker, then stopped. "I don't want to go through this again after lunch," she said. "It won't hurt to leave it unlocked during lunch, will it?"

"Nah," shrugged Mortimer. He clutched his stomach. "I just hope we have time for lunch. By the time we get to the cafeteria, the period will be over."

"I'll push the padlock up just enough to make it look as if it's closed all the way," Polly said. "There!" She turned to Mortimer. "Well, let's go before you lose your appetite," she laughed.

"Fat chance," said Mortimer as everyone headed for the cafeteria.

After lunch, the Clue Club returned to the hall. As they turned the corner, they saw an older boy leaning against Polly's locker. It was Allie Lime's brother, Ray. Allie's locker was next to Polly's.

"Will you tell my sister I left her soccer stuff in her locker?" Ray asked Polly. "I can't wait for her or I'll be late getting back to the high school."

"Sure," said Polly.

"Thanks," Ray said. He walked away then turned around. "I almost forgot," he called out. "Tell Allie I'll pick her up after soccer practice."

"Okay," Polly said, pulling on her padlock. The lock wouldn't move. "Oh no, my padlock is locked. I thought I left it open but I guess I closed it all the way by mistake." She tried the combination but the lock wouldn't open.

"Here, let me try," said Samantha.

"Pull on the lock, Sam," Georgie piped up.

"No!" yelled Polly.

"SSSSSHHH!" said Georgie. "You're making so much noise, Polly!"

"Me?" whispered Polly loudly. "You're the one who banged the lock before! Everyone in the fourth-grade wing heard that!"

Just then Allie Lime walked up. She turned her combination a couple of times before she got her locker open. When she looked inside, she wailed, "I knew he'd forget!"

"What's up, Allie?" asked Polly.

"I have soccer practice after school today and I forgot to bring my equipment," Allie said. "My brother was supposed to leave my soccer gear in my locker. I told him mine was third from the door, but I bet he forgot."

"No, he was here, Allie," said Polly. "He told me to tell you he left the soccer stuff. Oh, yeah, he also said he'd pick you up after practice."

"Well, I won't be going to practice because I have no gear," said Allie. "Someone must have taken it."

Samantha looked up from Polly's locker. "This thing is really stuck, Polly," she said.

"Why would anyone steal soccer equipment?" Wendy asked Allie.

"Maybe someone wanted my new cleats," said Allie.

"Does anyone else know your combination?" asked Peter.

"The only person who knows it is the kid who had this locker last year," said Allie.

She added, "Whoever had this locker last year could have opened it and taken my stuff."

"Everyone knows my combination," sighed Polly. "That's because everyone has tried to open it for me."

"Well, you don't have to worry about anybody stealing anything from yours, Polly," said Mortimer. "Even if someone knew the combination, they still couldn't get it open."

Allie looked into her locker again. "I don't believe it. She even took my team T-shirt! I was thinking about asking for a new combination padlock for my locker because it's so hard to open. Too bad I didn't do it."

"It's a good thing Polly's getting a new one today," said Samantha. "Mr. Gleamington is the only one who can get it open."

"Let me give it a spin," said Wendy. She bent down and put her ear to the lock. To everyone's shock, after one try the lock popped open.

"Hey, I know how you can make some money, Wendy," cried Georgie. "You can charge fourth graders to open their lockers!"

"Maybe she's already done that," Allie said, pointing to the bottom of Polly's locker. There was Allie's soccer gear.

"How'd this get in here?" cried Polly.

"What do you mean, how did it get in there, Polly?" Allie asked. "You knew my brother put the stuff in my locker. He must have left the door open or something. Anyhow, you took my soccer things."

"But Polly doesn't even play soccer," said Wendy.

"Yeah," said Georgie. "Why would she want your gear?"

"Don't ask me!" shouted Allie. "All I know is that my things are in her locker."

"Allie," said Polly, "you've got to believe me. I don't know how this got in here."

"Wait a minute," said Peter. "I think I

know what combination of events have caused this weird situation."

How did Allie's clothes get into Polly's locker? And how did Peter figure out what happened?

Solution
The Case of the Winning Combination

"Allie, you told your brother your locker was the third one from the door," explained Peter. "But you didn't tell him which door. Look."

The kids stepped back and looked at the lockers. In front of them was a row of six lockers. On either side of the row was a door. Allie's and Polly's lockers were in the middle of the row. That meant that both of their lockers were third from the door.

"Look!" cried Mortimer. "Polly's locker is third from the door, too."

"Except they are different doors," said Samantha.

"So my brother got the wrong locker," Allie said.

"Right," Peter went on. "He didn't have to use the combination to open it because Polly left it unlocked when she went to lunch."

"He put Allie's soccer gear inside Polly's

locker, then closed it up," finished Wendy.

"I'm sorry I accused you of stealing, Polly," said Allie.

"Don't worry about it," said Polly. "Luckily my friends and I are pretty good at solving mysteries."

"Looks as if this is an open-and-shut case," laughed Georgie.

3

The Case of the Ghost
Mystery

Georgie Green, Wendy White, and Samantha Scarlet were on their way to Peter Plum's house to meet Mortimer Mustard and Polly Peacock. From there, the Clue Club would be off to the Fall Festival!

Each year, around Halloween, the recreation department held the Fall Festival in Stewart Stadium. For one wonderful week, the playing field was crowded with rides, game booths, food stands, and even a haunted house.

"Next to Christmas, Halloween is my favorite holiday," said Georgie. "And the Fall Festival is like a whole week of Halloween."

"The haunted house is the best," said Wendy.

"I wonder if they have the Rocket Bomber ride again this year," said Samantha.

As the three kids rounded the corner to Peter's house, they spotted Mortimer and Polly coming from the other direction. Peter was standing on his front porch, waiting for everyone.

"Good timing!" Mortimer shouted.

"Yeah!" said Wendy. "And look! Peter's on time, too — for a change."

"Come on," Peter called to everyone. "Mr. Fairplay's giving us a ride." Peter pointed across the street to Mr. Fairplay, who was waving from his car.

Mr. Fairplay, Peter's neighbor, worked for the recreation department. When they arrived at the stadium, Mr. Fairplay said, "Would you like to see some of the offices where we run things?"

"Yeah!" exclaimed Georgie. "Can you show us where they control the scoreboard?"

"Sure," said Mr. Fairplay. "And how

about the booth where the radio announcers sit and broadcast the games?"

After a quick tour, the group headed towards Mr. Fairplay's office.

"You sure have a good view from the broadcast booth," exclaimed Wendy.

"If I don't make it as a football player, I'd like to run the scoreboard," said Georgie.

"Well, here's my office," said Mr. Fairplay. He pointed to a door that had MANAGER printed on it.

Several older kids were waiting inside. They were dressed up as ghosts.

"These ghosts are working for me this week," Mr. Fairplay said, smiling. He explained that he was in charge of hiring teenagers to work for the Fall Festival.

"What are the ghosts going to do?" asked Mortimer.

"They sell peanuts, Mortimer," answered Mr. Fairplay. "In fact, they are here to pick up their supplies." He pointed to a box on a table near his desk.

Mortimer looked in the box. It was filled with small bags of peanuts. Each bag was stamped with the slogan of the fair.

Mortimer held up a bag of peanuts. Samantha read the slogan out loud. "Support Recreation!"

"The rec department gets its supplies from a special dealer," said Mr. Fairplay. "The soda cups have that slogan printed on them, too. It reminds people that the money they spend is going to a good cause."

"I'll be a ghost for you anytime!" said Georgie.

"That's the spirit," chuckled Mr. Fairplay. "Well, you kids go on out and enjoy yourselves. I'll see you back here when the festival is over tonight."

The kids ran out to the field where people were walking around.

"Mr. Fairplay says I can sell peanuts at the festival when I'm old enough," Peter told the others.

"Speaking of peanuts," said Georgie. He

walked over to a ghost standing by the merry-go-round and asked for a bag.

"Here you go," the ghost said, handing him some peanuts. "That's fifty cents."

"Look," he said. He held the bag up over his head as if it were a heavy weight. "I'm supporting the rec department, get it?"

"Come on, guys," laughed Peter. "Let's go on the bumper cars."

The kids had so much fun on the bumper cars that they rode them three times. Afterwards, Mortimer, who was always hungry, asked Georgie if he had any more peanuts.

"Are you kidding?" asked Georgie. "They're long gone."

"Hey, there's another ghost," said Polly. "You can get your own bag."

After Mortimer bought his peanuts, he wanted to ride the Ferris wheel.

"Not me," said Polly. "I'm afraid of heights. Who wants to go on the Rocket Bomber instead?"

"The Rocket Bomber!" exclaimed Peter.

"You're upside down for the whole ride. How can you be afraid of the Ferris wheel and not the Rocket Bomber?"

"Because on the Ferris wheel you're just sitting in the middle of the air," said Polly. "There's nothing around you. Then my car always stops at the very top forever."

"But at least you're not stuck upside down," Peter said.

"Come on, Georgie," Polly said. "You go on the Rocket Bomber with me."

Georgie's grin disappeared. "Oooo, not me," he said. "That ride really scares me."

Now it was Polly's turn to grin. "Anyone else want to come?" she asked.

"Absolutely not," Samantha said. "I hate those kinds of rides."

"I'd throw up," said Peter.

"I could handle the Rocket Bomber, of course," said Mortimer, looking down at his feet. "But I'd rather ride the Ferris wheel."

Polly and Wendy went on the Rocket Bomber while the others rocked on top of

33

the Ferris wheel. Then Polly and Wendy went on the Scrambler, the Centrifugal Force Machine, and the Rocky Roller Coaster.

After they got off the roller coaster, Polly cried, "We've saved the best for last. Now let's all go through the haunted house!"

The six friends shrieked through the haunted house and came out the back door, laughing and screaming.

"Yuk," said Mortimer. "I touched brains!"

"I was really really scared for a minute in the basement," admitted Polly.

"She's scared of the haunted house and the Ferris wheel, but not the Rocket Bomber," said Georgie, shaking his head. "I just don't get it."

Finally it was nearly time for the Fall Festival to close up for the evening. The kids had gone on every ride and stuffed themselves on cotton candy, caramel apples, hot cider, and more peanuts.

"I guess we should head back to Mr. Fairplay's office," said Peter. Just then the kids saw Mr. Fairplay heading toward them. Three police officers were with him.

"What's the matter?" Peter asked.

"You may have to call your parents to pick you up tonight," Mr. Fairplay said. "Looks like I'll be here a while."

"What's wrong?" asked Polly.

"Several people have reported seeing a pickpocket," explained one of the police officers. "They say it's one of the peanut vendors."

"There are ten ghosts selling peanuts," Mr. Fairplay told the kids. "We're going to have to try to find all of them before the thief gets away."

"I'll bet I can pick out the pickpocket," Wendy said. "Follow me."

"Where are we going?" asked Mr. Fairplay.

"To the bumper cars," replied Wendy.

"This is no time to go on a ride, Wendy," said Mr. Fairplay.

When they reached the bumper cars, Wendy walked up to a ghost selling peanuts and pointed to him. "There's your pickpocket," she declared.

"How can you tell, Wendy?" asked Mr. Fairplay.

How does Wendy know which ghost is the thief?

Solution
The Case of the Ghost Mystery

"His peanuts gave him away," explained Wendy.

"What?" said the boy.

"He's not selling the recreation department's peanuts," said Wendy. "Those packages have the slogan, Support Recreation. Look on his bag, Mr. Fairplay."

"That's right!" exclaimed Mortimer. "I remember. I bought a pack from you. The bag of peanuts you were selling said Plenty Peanuts."

"He made his own ghost costume so he would look like the other peanut sellers," said Polly.

The ghost vendor looked down at the floor. He confessed to everything. "I hid the wallets behind the bleachers in section J," he told Mr. Fairplay.

"Fred, could you go pick up the wallets?"

Mr. Fairplay asked a police officer. Then he turned to the Clue Club kids. "A lot of people with missing wallets are grateful to you kids," he said.

"Around us, thieves don't have a ghost of a chance!" laughed Georgie.

4

The Case of the Missing Movie

A large group of kids were standing outside Goodview Video, the town's video store. Tonight the Mystery Movie Club was meeting. The club was waiting to see the movie of Agatha Christie's book *And Then There Were None*.

"Next to the Clue Club, the Mystery Movie Club is the greatest," said Samantha Scarlet.

"This is one of your best ideas yet, Wendy," said Mortimer Mustard.

"Wendy, it was a brilliant idea!" Peter Plum said.

"Well, it was really Mrs. Goodview's idea," said Wendy White.

Mrs. Goodview was the owner of Goodview Videos. One day, after Wendy checked out a mystery video, she told Mrs. Good-view about the Clue Club.

"Mrs. Goodview said she was a mystery lover, too," said Wendy. "And she asked me if I thought some kids would like to form a Mystery Movie Club. She has a small screening room behind her store, and she said she would let the club watch movies there once a month. You guys helped me with the rest."

"Well, the flyers I made for you on my computer were rather good," said Peter Plum.

"They were," agreed Georgie Green. "But it was my message that grabbed the kids' attention."

"Yeah, Georgie," said Polly Peacock. "I'm trying to forget, I mean, remember what it said."

"You don't have to remember," said Georgie. "There's a copy of it in the store window."

The kids turned to the window and looked at the sign. It read:

WHAT DO YOU GET
WHEN MYSTERY MOVIE LOVERS GET
TOGETHER?
THE MYSTERY MOVIE CLUB!

"Oh, well," said Wendy. "It doesn't matter what the flyer says. It seems like everybody in school wants to join."

"Yeah, so many kids joined up, Mrs. Goodview had to divide the club into grades," said Peter.

"She's having an Agatha Christie festival," said Polly excitedly.

"Tonight's movie is *And Then There Were None*," said Mortimer. "And the next one is *The Alphabet Murders*."

Mrs. Goodview came out the door of the video store. "Come this way," she told the kids. Once everyone was inside, she pointed toward a door in the back of the store.

"Right through there is the screening room. There's a big-screen TV and comfortable seats," she said. "Help yourselves to popcorn and drinks." As soon as everyone was settled into their seats, Mrs. Goodview came in and started the video.

Afterwards, everyone stood in the store for a minute talking about the movie.

"Wasn't it smart the way the murderer pretended to be killed?" said Wendy.

"Yeah," agreed Mortimer. "No one would suspect a dead person of doing anything."

"Why don't we wait outside for my mom, so Mrs. Goodview can close up," said Samantha. Mrs. Scarlet was giving the Clue Club kids a ride home.

"Thanks for letting us have our meeting here, Mrs. Goodview," Mortimer said.

"It gives me an excuse to watch these movies myself," said Mrs. Goodview. "Well, I'm going to rewind the tape and close up. Good night, now."

On their way out of the store, the kids noticed a bike leaning against the side of the building.

"Hey, Donny, isn't that your brother's

bike?" asked Peter. Donny Claret was in the Clue Club's fourth-grade class, as well as the Mystery Movie Club. His brother Carl was in the eighth grade.

Donny looked around. "Where?" he asked. Then he saw the bike. "Oh . . . yeah, that's Carl's bike," he said. "I rode it here."

He pulled the bike away from the wall and walked off down the street. "Well, see you tomorrow, guys," he called out.

"Bye," everyone called out to Donny. "So long."

"You'd never know Donny and Carl were brothers," said Wendy.

"Yeah, one is so good and one is so bad," said Polly.

"That too," said Wendy. "But I was going to say one has dark hair and the other is blond."

"Plus Donny is quiet and Carl is always getting into trouble," said Samantha. "The only thing that's important to Carl is basketball."

"Wonder when I'll get my growth spurt," sighed Georgie. "I know a few more inches would help me play as well as Carl."

Samantha's mother drove up to the curb. "It's a good thing none of us is any taller," said Samantha, as everyone piled into the car. "Otherwise the whole Clue Club couldn't fit into our car."

At school the next morning, Mr. Higgins, the principal, called the Mystery Movie Club into his office. Mrs. Goodview was there, too.

"Boys and girls," Mr. Higgins said, "I have some upsetting news. I've just been informed that several videos were taken from Goodview Videos last night. None of the locks were broken so it looks as if someone came in during the Mystery Movie Club meeting."

Just then, Carl Claret walked into the office.

"I've asked Carl to come, too, because I understand his bike was seen behind the store," Mr. Higgins told them. "Carl, would you mind telling me why you were at the video store last night?"

"I wasn't," Carl said rudely. "I was at home all night. My brother borrowed my bike to go to his stupid Mystery Movie Club."

"Is this true, Donald?" asked Mr. Higgins.

Donny looked at his older brother. "Yes sir," he answered.

Then Mr. Higgins asked, "Mrs. Goodview, did any of the children leave during the meeting last evening?"

"Well, let's see," said Mrs. Goodview. "Mortimer Mustard asked to be excused once. I believe everyone else was in the screening room the whole time."

"And did all the children leave the store at the same time?" Mr. Higgins asked.

"I walked them to the front door myself," Mrs. Goodview answered. "Then I went back to the screening room to rewind the video and turn out the lights. I left right after that and locked up behind me.

No one could have taken the videos after I left. This morning when I put our movie back on the shelf I noticed that several others were missing."

"Well, I guess everyone can go but Mortimer," said Mr. Higgins.

"But I didn't take the videos, Mr. Higgins!" cried Mortimer.

"Excuse me, Mr. Higgins," said Georgie. "Mortimer didn't do it, but I know who did."

Who took the videos? And how does Georgie know?

simple matter to prove what Georgie is saying."

"All right, I took 'em," said Carl. "I knew Donny's club was meeting at the store last night. So I snuck in and grabbed a few movies. But everybody came out before I could get away."

"Donny figured out something was wrong. He pretended that he rode your bike over to cover for you," said Peter.

"Looks like your growth spurt helped you in basketball," Mortimer told Carl, "and it helped us catch you in a lie."

Solution
The Case of the Missing Movie

"What do you know about this, Georgie?" said Mr. Higgins. "Well, speak up, boy."

"Mr. Higgins, if Carl and Donny will stand beside each other, I can show you," said Georgie. When the two brothers stood side by side, Carl was almost two feet taller than his little brother.

"Donny didn't ride your bike to the video store, Carl. He couldn't have," said Georgie.

"Donny is so much shorter than his brother, his legs won't reach the pedals of Carl's bike," said Wendy.

"That's right," said Polly. "I remember Donny walked off with the bike last night. He didn't ride it."

"You must have been at the video store last night, Carl," said Georgie.

"What about this, Carl?" said Mr. Higgins sternly. "Tell the truth, son. It's a

The Case of the Stolen Starter

Mortimer Mustard and Georgie Green were having a very serious discussion on the playground after school.

"Georgie, you've got to come with me," Mortimer pleaded. "I can't go through this alone."

"Mortimer, you're only going to have your teeth cleaned," said Georgie.

"Don't forget about the cavity," Mortimer said. He shuddered.

"One tiny cavity," Georgie sighed. "Your mother said it was so small, you don't even need any Novocaine."

"No Novocaine!" screeched Mortimer. "You've got to be kidding."

Just then, Wendy White and Samantha Scarlet walked up.

"Mortimer has to go to the dentist today," Georgie told them.

"Someone has to go with me," moaned Mortimer.

"Oh, Mortimer," said Samanatha.

Wendy smiled at Mortimer. "I think going to the dentist is scary, too," she said. "I'd go with you, but I have a violin lesson."

Wendy saw Peter Plum and Polly Peacock heading toward them. "There's Peter and Polly," she said. "Maybe one of them can go."

"Hey, guys," called Peter. He and Polly looked at Mortimer's face. "What's up?" Peter asked him.

"Yeah. What's wrong with you, Mortimer?" asked Polly.

"His teeth," said Samantha. "Can one of you go with him to the dentist?"

"Mortimer, you are too much." Polly shook her head. "Sorry, I can't go. My mom is taking me to get new sneakers."

"My dentist will let you watch," Mortimer said to Peter. "Would you like to see how a cavity is filled?"

Peter perked up. He couldn't resist the chance to learn something. "Well, as a matter of fact, I would like to see that," Peter said. "Okay, I'll come, Mortimer."

"Hey, I'd like to see that," said Georgie. "Maybe I'll come along, too."

"Great!" exclaimed Mortimer. "Dr. Toth won't mind if I bring two friends. But no jokes, Georgie. Okay?"

"Hey, I can't help it," said Georgie. "You open your mouth and there's a cavity. I open my mouth and there's a joke."

"At least the dentist can fix Mortimer's cavities," said Polly. "No one can help your bad jokes, Georgie." Everyone laughed.

"All right, all right," Mortimer said. "We better go or I'll be late. Then I'll have to sit in the waiting room and listen to the dentist's drill." He shuddered again.

The boys arrived at the dentist's office right on time for Mortimer's appointment. The office was in a large building with many offices. Dr. Toth took them into the examination room, and Peter and Georgie watched her clean Mortimer's teeth.

Mortimer kept his eyes closed while Dr. Toth drilled and filled the tooth. He still had them closed after she had removed the cotton and the tube.

"You can open your eyes now, Mortimer," Dr. Toth said. "We're all finished." Mortimer blinked his eyes and smiled.

Dr. Toth walked the boys to the waiting room. She gave Mortimer some instructions. "Now, Mortimer, don't eat anything for an hour," Dr. Toth said.

Mortimer nodded his head.

"No chewing on that side tonight," Dr. Toth told him.

The boys walked over to the coatrack in the waiting room. "My new starter jacket," Peter cried. "It's not here."

"What's wrong?" asked Dr. Toth.

"I hung my Padres jacket on the coatrack, and now it's gone," Peter told her. "This is only the third time I've worn it."

"Quick! Let's see if anyone's in the hall," said Georgie. The boys checked the hall, the elevator, and the ground floor of the building. There was no sign of anyone or any jacket. They trooped back up to Dr. Toth's office.

"I guess I better call my mom to come get us," Peter told her sadly. "It's too cold to walk home without a coat."

The next day, Peter had to wear his old coat to school. When he met the kids that morning in the school yard, he had a long face.

"I feel really bad, Peter," said Mortimer. "If you hadn't gone with me to the dentist, you would still have your coat."

"It's not your fault," said Peter.

Everyone felt very glum. They stood in silence, waiting for the bell to ring. Suddenly Polly exclaimed, "Look, Peter, Sammy's wearing a new Padres starter jacket." She pointed to Sammy Sage standing on the other side of the playground.

"I know Sammy wanted a starter

jacket," Peter told the other kids. "He told me the first day I wore mine. But he said that his parents wouldn't buy him one because they just got him a new winter coat for Christmas."

The kids walked over to Sammy. "I see you got a starter jacket after all," Peter said to him. "How come your parents changed their minds?"

"They got a good deal on this one," said Sammy. "Well, I gotta go. I don't want to be late for class."

"The bell hasn't rung yet," said Georgie. "What's your hurry?"

"Peter's starter jacket got stolen yesterday at the doctor's office," said Mortimer.

"Say, you weren't in the office were you, Sammy?" asked Peter.

"No, Plum. I wasn't near that dentist's office yesterday or the day before or the day before that," snapped Sammy. "You've got a nerve accusing me of stealing your jacket. There are other kids in town

who have a Padres starter jacket. Why don't you go ask them?"

"I think we already have the answer," said Wendy. "You took the jacket, all right."

"Prove it then," yelled Sammy.

How does Wendy know Sammy took Peter's starter jacket from Dr. Toth's office?

Solution
The Case of the Stolen Starter

"You said it yourself, Sammy," replied Wendy.

"What do you mean?" said Sammy. "I didn't say a thing."

"No, it was us who didn't say a thing," explained Wendy. "At least no one said anything about where the jacket was lost."

"Hey, that's right!" exclaimed Polly. "Peter said he lost it at the *doctor's* office. How did you know the doctor was a dentist, Sammy?"

"The only way you could have known that is if you were there," said Samantha.

The Clue Club surrounded Sammy. "And you'd better give it back right now." Wendy glared at Sammy.

Sammy had no choice. He took off the jacket and gave it to Peter.

"This is one case that barely got started!" Georgie said.

6

The Case of
Foul Play at the Fair

The school playground was full of excitement. Everyone wanted to know who would win first prize in the Spring Science Fair.

During the week, each grade visited the science room to see the exhibits. Every boy and girl in the school had an opinion about which one would win. The judges were coming to look at the science projects and award a prize to one student in each grade.

The Clue Club was talking on the playground before school. There had been a thunderstorm the night before. It had left little puddles of water on the school yard blacktop. The wind had blown some tree limbs off the nearby trees, and several branches were lying on the school grounds.

"That was some storm last night," exclaimed Polly Peacock. "It was very exciting!"

"Exciting?" shrieked Samantha Scarlet. "It was scary! I didn't sleep all night. Look at all the branches it blew down."

"I think thunderstorms are exciting, too," said Wendy White.

"Speaking of exciting, the science fair judges are coming today," Georgie Green said.

"Peter's talking trash can is pretty clever," said Mortimer Mustard. Peter Plum had hooked up a tape recorder inside a trash can. When the lid was lifted, it turned the tape recorder on. The tape told how recycling helped save the world's resources.

"It's supposed to inspire people to recycle," Peter said.

"Hey, what about Samantha's evaporator?" asked Wendy.

"It's great, too," said Polly. "But I think

we all know who's going to win first prize in fourth grade this year."

"Yeah," said Mortimer. "Wendy."

This year Wendy came up with something extra special. It was a miniature windmill made out of wood and tiny bricks. When the wheel turned, it moved two stones that could actually grind grain.

Wendy's project included a fan that blew on the wheel to turn it. But Ms. Mocha, the science teacher, wanted to use real wind. So she asked Wendy to set up the windmill near a window so that the spring breeze would blow in and turn the wheel.

"Your windmill is perfect, Wendy," exclaimed Polly. "And it's really different. You should win first prize this year."

"I really want to," said Wendy shyly.

"So does Pam Pinkerton," said Samantha. "In fact, she told me she thinks her volcano project will definitely win."

"I think Wendy's windmill is the best," said Polly.

"How did you come up with that idea?" Peter asked Wendy.

"Over lunch with Petunia," answered Wendy. "I was eating a cheese sandwich on whole wheat bread and Petunia was eating her parrot seed. I was watching her crack the seeds in her beak. I realized that we were kind of eating the same thing."

"Cheese?" said Mortimer.

"No, grains," replied Wendy. "Only Petunia was grinding up her grain and my grain was already ground up into bread. Anyway, that's when I got the idea to make a windmill."

"I can just hear your speech when the judges hand you your prize," said Georgie. "I'd like to thank my pet parrot, Petunia, for her inspiration." Everyone laughed at the thought of Wendy saying that.

"Let's go see if the judges are here yet," said Samantha. "We have time before the bell rings."

When the kids entered the science room, they found Wendy's windmill lying on the floor. The beautiful wheel was bent. Pam Pinkerton was standing near the table where the windmill had been sitting. The Clue Club kids ran over to the table.

"My windmill is ruined!" cried Wendy.

"Wow!" exclaimed Mortimer. "What happened, Pam?"

"The wind blew in and knocked it off the table," said Pam. "I tried to catch it, but I couldn't reach it in time."

"We opened the window yesterday so that the wind could turn your mill," said Ms. Mocha. "But I thought I closed it last night."

"The window was open when I came in," said Pam.

"This is a real shame, Wendy," Ms. Mocha said. "I don't know if you have time to fix your windmill before the judges get here."

"I'm sorry, Wendy," said Pam.

"It's not your fault," said Wendy, trying to hold back her tears.

"Oh, yes, it is your fault, Pam," ex-

claimed Peter angrily. "You knocked Wendy's windmill over so you could win the science prize."

How does Peter know Pam knocked over Wendy's windmill?

Mocha and smiled. "That is, if Ms. Mocha will let us skip science class," he said.

"All right, Mortimer," said Ms. Mocha, laughing. "I guess this is a good reason to miss class."

Then Ms. Mocha looked at Pam, who was hanging her head. "Pam, I'm sorry but I'll have to disqualify your project from the science fair because of what you've done."

"Looks like you blew it when you tried to be the wind, Pam," said Georgie.

Solution
The Case of Foul Play at the Fair

"That's a harsh thing to accuse someone of, Peter," said Ms. Mocha. "Why do you think Pam did this?"

"Look where the windmill fell," Peter said.

"It's on the wrong side of the table!" exclaimed Polly.

"Right," said Peter. "It's *between* the table and the window. It couldn't have landed there unless the wind had inhaled."

"I see," said Georgie. "If the wind had blown the windmill off, it would have landed on the other side of the table — away from the window."

"You did push it off, Pam," said Ms. Mocha sternly. "You lied."

Mortimer bent down to inspect the broken windmill. "I think we can repair your windmill before the judges get here, Wendy," he said. Then he looked up at Ms.

The Case of the Mad Dog

The Clue Club was having its Saturday meeting at Peter Plum's house. It was almost lunchtime, but the Clue Jr. game was so exciting that no one cared. Even Mortimer Mustard wasn't grumbling about his empty stomach — and Mortimer was always hungry.

Peter was the only one who couldn't keep his mind on the game. He kept looking at his watch, but not because it was time to eat. Peter was checking his watch because it was time for the mail to come. In fact, it was past time. Mr. Post, the letter carrier, was late.

"Peter!" said Mortimer. "Pay attention! You just missed a clue."

"I'm sorry," Peter told Mortimer. "I'm

waiting for the mail. My new mystery magazine should be here today."

"Oh, yeah," said Georgie Green. "It's called *I Spy*, right?"

"Ooooh," exclaimed Polly Peacock. "I've heard about it. It has lists of new books and movie reviews — and some mystery stories, too."

"It's so late, I'm afraid Mr. Post isn't coming," said Peter. "Maybe we didn't get any mail today."

"Why don't we take the Clue Jr. game out to the porch. We can play while we watch for Mr. Post," Wendy White suggested.

"I think we have to," agreed Samantha Scarlet. "Peter won't be able to keep his mind on anything until he gets that magazine."

The kids picked up their game and moved it to the front porch. Peter threw the ball to his dog, Bizzy, while the others played Clue Jr. It wasn't too long before they heard Mr. Post whistling down the block.

"Here he comes!" cried Peter. He ran to the fence that went around the Plums' yard.

"Hello, son," said Mr. Post, as he walked through the front gate. He handed Peter the mail. "You looking for this?"

"Here it is," Peter exclaimed. "The new *I Spy*!" He held up the magazine for the other kids to see. Just then Bizzy jumped up and grabbed the magazine from Peter's hand. Then he began chewing on it.

"Stop, Bizzy!" shrieked Peter. "No, boy!"

When Peter finally got the magazine back, part of it was in shreds. "Oh, no! Look at this," Peter cried. "Bizzy, what's with you?"

But Bizzy wasn't paying any attention to his master. As soon as Peter got the magazine away, Bizzy jumped up on Mr. Post, knocking him down. Then Bizzy began clawing at the mailbag.

"Aaaaah!" screamed Mr. Post. "Get him off me!"

Peter grabbed Bizzy's collar and pulled his dog back. "What are you doing, Bizzy?" he yelled.

Peter held Bizzy while Polly and Georgie helped Mr. Post get up.

"Here's your hat, Mr. Post," said Samantha. When Mr. Post took his hat, his hands were shaking. He brushed himself off, then turned to Peter.

"This time Bizzy has gone too far!" Mr. Post said. "Your dog has jumped at me before but it was always friendly. He's never knocked me down. I'm afraid I need to speak to your parents."

"Polly, could you get my dad?" Peter asked. "I need to hold Bizzy."

"Sure," said Polly. She ran to the front door and called Peter's dad.

When Mr. Plum came out, Mr. Post spoke to him very seriously.

"Mr. Plum, your dog has attacked me," Mr. Post told him. "From now on, I want you to put him in the garage when I deliver the mail."

"I'm sorry, Mr. Post," Mr. Plum said. "Bizzy's never acted like that before." Everyone looked down at Bizzy. He was still straining to get at Mr. Post. Peter was having a hard time holding him back.

Suddenly Mr. Post looked worried. "Your dog isn't sick, is he?" he asked. "Is Bizzy a mad dog? If he has rabies, he'll have to be put to sleep, you know." He looked at his hands, then he felt his face. "I hope he didn't bite me," he muttered.

At that, Peter's mouth dropped open.

"Why don't you come inside and sit a moment, Mr. Post," said Mr. Plum. While Mr. Plum tried to calm Mr. Post down, the Clue Club gang pulled Bizzy to the back of the house.

Peter tied Bizzy to his leash. He sat on the ground and hugged his dog. "Don't worry, Bizzy," he said. "We won't put you to sleep." He looked up at the others. "You don't think Bizzy's a mad dog, do you?"

"No," said Samantha. "But what he did was really strange."

"It sure was," agreed Georgie. "Why did Bizzy just start jumping on Mr. Post, anyway?"

"Something else is odd," said Wendy. "Why did Bizzy try to eat the *I Spy* magazine?"

The kids put fresh water in Bizzy's bowl and watched the dog for a few minutes. Bizzy looked at them looking at him for a while. When the kids didn't do anything, Bizzy yawned. Then he took a drink from his water bowl, flopped down, and went to sleep.

"Bizzy doesn't seem mad to me," shrugged Samantha.

"Nope, this is pretty normal behavior," agreed Peter. The kids walked back around to the front of the house and sat on the front porch. They could hear Mr. Plum and Mr. Post talking in the living room. The two men were discussing what to do with Bizzy.

"This is awful," said Peter. "I'm worried. Bizzy's never chased anyone, except in fun."

"He almost ruined your new magazine," said Mortimer. He picked up the *I Spy* and began to leaf through the pages. Some crumbs fell out of the magazine onto his lap. "Yuk!" Mortimer said. "This magazine is full of crumbs."

Polly took the magazine. "It smells funny, too," she said, wrinkling up her nose.

"Yeah," said Wendy, coming over to sniff. "Almost like some kind of food."

"Not any food I would eat," said Mortimer.

"Well, if *you* wouldn't eat it, no human would," laughed Georgie.

The kids looked up as Mr. Plum and Mr. Post came through the front door.

"We'll keep an eye on Bizzy," Mr. Plum told Mr. Post.

"Thank you," said Mr. Post. "Just keep him tied up when I make my rounds." Mr.

Post walked toward his bag, which was still on the ground. Polly ran over to help him pick it up. But before Mr. Post could put the bag on his shoulder, Polly stuck her head inside and sniffed loudly.

"Polly," exclaimed Mr. Post. "What on earth are you doing?"

"Mr. Post," Polly said, "I don't think Bizzy attacked you."

"What do you mean, he didn't attack me?" said Mr. Post angrily. "You kids are witnesses. You saw him jump on me yourself."

"I think the big mystery is *why* he jumped on you, Mr. Post," continued Polly. "And I think the answer is in your mailbag."

What made Bizzy jump on Mr. Post? And why does Polly think it's in the mailbag?

Solution
The Case of the Mad Dog

"Well, all right," said Mr. Post. "It can't hurt to look." Mr. Post took out everything in his mailbag. At the bottom was a small package with a hole in it, and a couple of little bone-shaped cookies.

"These cookies probably fell out of that open box," said Mr. Post. "Let's see what the label on the package says."

Mr. Post read the label out loud: "Daring Dog Dishes. Guaranteed to Increase Your Dog's Appetite."

"Why, it's dog food!" Mr. Plum exclaimed. "High-powered dog food."

"That's why Bizzy jumped on you," said Peter. "He was trying to get the dog food."

"How did you know, Polly?" asked Samantha.

"Well, remember how Bizzy was trying to eat your new *I Spy*?" Polly asked. "Then Mortimer found crumbs in it. And it smelled, too. It was sort of a food smell.

When I sniffed Mr. Post's bag, it smelled the same as the magazine. I knew something in the bag made the magazine smell. And that's what Bizzy was trying to get."

"Well, it's a relief to know that Bizzy's not a mad dog," Peter said, smiling happily. He hugged Bizzy tightly.

"No, he's just mad about dog food," Georgie laughed.

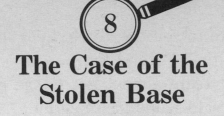

The Case of the
Stolen Base

Little League season was nearly over, and Georgie Green's team was in the final playoffs. Georgie played first base for the Signs, the team sponsored by the local store, Signature Signs. The Signs had just finished a game against the Wigs, a team sponsored by the Wigs for All Occasions store.

Both teams had a 9–2 record for the reg ular season. Whichever team won two out of three playoff games would win the championship. The Wigs won the first game. And the Signs had just won the second game today.

The Clue Club kids had come to cheer for Georgie. After the game they met him at the refreshment stand.

"I hate to see the Little League season end," sighed Peter Plum.

"Your team almost got to the playoffs, Peter," said Samantha Scarlet.

Mortimer Mustard rubbed his hands together. "It would have been great to see Peter and Georgie both in the playoffs," he said.

"Remember when the Wigs shortstop almost stole home today?" Georgie asked. He began to imitate what the Signs pitcher and catcher had done to stop the run. In his excitement, he accidentally smeared mustard from his hot dog on his glove.

Polly Peacock sighed. "Georgie, how can you make such neat catches on first base and still be such a slob? Everything you own has mustard or ketchup or some kind of stain on it."

"Georgie just gets too excited to be careful," said Wendy White.

"Everyone is going to Samantha's house to watch a mystery movie," Polly said. "Hurry up, Georgie."

Georgie walked over to the pile of bat bags and stuffed his glove into his bag. Then he walked back to the refreshment stand. "One hot dog with extra mustard, please," he told the woman behind the counter. Then he looked at Polly and giggled. Polly rolled her eyes.

"Okay, let's go," Georgie said. He crammed the last bite of hot dog into his mouth and wiped his mouth on his sleeve. "Uh-oh," he said, looking at the yellow smear on his sleeve. "I did it again." He jogged over to the fence before Polly could say anything and threw his bat bag onto his shoulder.

The next day the kids met at Georgie's house. Mr. Green said he would give them a ride to the baseball field.

"Well, it's the final game of the playoffs," said Peter eagerly.

"Are you nervous, Georgie?" asked Samantha.

"Nah," Georgie replied. "I'm too good to be nervous."

He unzipped his bat bag to put a bottle of water inside. "My glove! It's gone!" he wailed. "Someone must have taken it yesterday while I was having another hot dog."

"And right before the playoffs," said Peter. "That's some bad luck. Well, Georgie, you can use mine. It's a Ken Griffey, Jr."

"Thanks, Peter," said Georgie. "I won't be used to it, but it'll be better than no glove."

Mr. Green drove everyone to Peter's house to pick up his glove. By the time they reached the baseball field, Georgie was almost late.

"Now I'm nervous," Georgie said to Samantha.

"You'll do fine, son," his dad told him. "A glove isn't what makes a good player."

That day, the game was close all the way. Georgie fumbled the ball twice at first base because he was not used to Peter's mitt. In between innings the kids brought him a candy bar, but he was so upset, he couldn't eat it.

"We're going to lose because of me," Georgie told them.

"First base is a very important position," said Peter wisely. "But no baseball game was ever lost by one player."

"Yeah, but it's the top of the ninth and the score is 6–7, Wigs favor," moaned Georgie. "If I had my own glove, I know I could have gotten at least one of those runners out."

"Georgie, you're up next!" the coach called out.

"Maybe I can bring our score up," Georgie said, as he pulled on his batting gloves.

On the second pitch, Georgie hit a ground ball and made it to first. On the next pitch, the Wigs catcher fumbled the ball and Georgie decided to steal second. When the catcher threw the ball to Susan Slate on second, Georgie slid. Susan tagged Georgie, but she was too late. The umpire hollered, "SAAAFE!"

As he was getting to his feet, Georgie noticed that Susan's baseball glove had a yellow stain on it.

"That's my glove!" shouted Georgie.

"Right," Susan said. "And you're Babe Ruth. Don't try to distract me, Georgie. I know you want to win but that's not the way."

"Neither is swiping my glove," Georgie muttered. Just then there was another hit and Georgie had to run to third. Then the third base coach waved him home. He almost didn't make it across the plate in time because he was so busy looking at Susan's glove.

Georgie's run tied the score 7–7, and the Signs scored one more run, making it 8–7. After the Wigs were scoreless in the bottom of the ninth, the Signs had won the game and the championship.

Amid all the celebrating afterwards,

Georgie made his way over to Susan Slate. "That's my glove!" he yelled. "If I hadn't stolen second base, I wouldn't have noticed that you had it."

"What are you talking about, Georgie? This is my glove," said Susan. "See? It's my Cal Ripkin."

"Yes, I see," said Georgie, "I had one too — and mine has a mustard stain on it. Does yours?"

The Clue Club had followed Georgie and were looking at Susan's glove.

"The fact that you're a slob definitely proves that this is your glove, Georgie," Polly said. "Believe me, that's his glove, Susan. Look at this stain." Polly pointed to a yellow spot.

"Georgie dropped mustard on his glove yesterday when he was eating a hot dog," Wendy added. "We all saw him."

"Well, this glove does have a stain on it," Susan admitted. "But I didn't steal his glove. Why should I? I have one."

"To help your team win, that's why!"

yelled Georgie. "You know I play first base. You took my glove so I'd be catching with one I wasn't used to. I dropped a couple of balls, too, because of that. You wanted us to lose the game. I tell you, she stole my glove."

"I don't think Susan stole your glove, Georgie," Samantha said.

How does Samantha know that Susan didn't take Georgie's glove? And what happened?

Solution
The Case of the Stolen Base

"How can you say that?" Georgie asked.

"You picked up Susan's bag by mistake when we were leaving the softball field yesterday," said Samantha. "They look the same. You probably put your glove in it by mistake, too."

"But Susan checked her bag," said Mortimer. "She knew it was hers when she saw her Cal Ripkin glove."

"Samantha, are you saying she actually found Georgie's glove and thought it was hers?" Wendy asked.

"That's right," said Samantha. "Let's look in Susan's bag again."

Susan opened her bag and sure enough there was her glove.

"Well, Georgie, your team didn't lose because you lost your glove," said Mortimer. "And you didn't actually lose your glove."

"Looks like there are no losers at the end of this case," laughed Georgie.